R.J. LAMP POST

A DAY IN THE LIFE

BY
VIRGINIA M. LAWRENCE

(Coach Gran)

R. J. Lamp Post
(A Day In The Life)

Meet R.J. Lamp Post

Hey! How ya doin'? My name is Reggie Lamp Post. My mom and pops call me 'Junior' 'cause I am, you know! Named after my father, almost everyone calls me R.J. You get it? R for Reggie and J for Junior. Yes? No? Whatever!

Anyway, I've got my pops' old job now. He worked it for 48 long years. After nearly 50 years on the job, Pops was old and rusted, so he retired. When he did, I asked him, "Pops, how about giving me a few tips or pointers on how to do a good job?"

"Junior, you don't have to worry about a thing," he said. "You're made for the job! You're built with the newest, toughest, rust-resistant alloy there is. You're taller, stronger, and designed to repel lightning bolts. You can handle the hottest summer temperatures, rain, high winds, snow, blizzards, and the coldest winters. Boy! When you think about it, you're almost like Superman!"

R J "Superman" Lamp Post!

Wouldn't Wanna Be Rodney

Of course, you wouldn't have to deal with all of that if you had taken that job in Phoenix instead of staying in Michigan. Or you could have taken that transformer pole job.

You mean like Rodney, who stands on the side street near the back of Mrs. Lowrv's house? Rodney has wires leading into his pole and wires leading away from it—all kinds of wires. They could be electrical wires, telephone wires, or cable wires. Any kind of wires!

You know what happened the other night? There was this really powerful thunderstorm. It was raining cats and dogs, with periodic flashes of lightning and really, really loud booms of thunder. A bolt of lightning struck Rodney.

Even though it was 9:30 p.m. and dark, that lightning strike lit up the sky like it was daylight. Sparks were flying everywhere as the lightning sliced the main electrical wire.

Rodney struck by lightning
Live electrical wire down

That wire dropped onto the roof of Mrs. Lowry's metal garage. It bounced around the roof a few times, then swung down along the side of the garage and landed on her metal chain-link fence. It electrified the fence before falling to the ground at the foot of Rodney's pole. It was emitting a pulsating yellow and orange glow; it looked like something was on fire. The path of that live wire along the side of the garage was marked by a streak of black scorch marks with a line of various-sized, bullet-like holes. It looked like someone had riddled the side of Mrs. Lowry's garage with an automatic Uzi rifle.

That was some mean electricity; it made those holes while darting in and out of the garage. It fried the garage's electrical wiring system, shattered the lightbulb into smithereens, and blew out the automatic garage door opener. It could have set Rodney on fire since Rodney is wooden. Yes, he's made of wood! But I suppose the heavy rain would have doused the fire.

The Real Bad Guy
(Lightning vs Thunder)

That thunderstorm was the most horrific and amazing phenomenon of nature I have ever seen. But I wonder why it's called a thunderstorm. Basically, thunder is just sound; granted, a really, really loud rumbling noise, but it is virtually harmless. Thunder is merely the sound lightning makes. Lightning is the real culprit! The real bad guy!

THUNDER

KABOOM

LIGHTNING

As our esteemed founding father Ben Franklin discovered, lightning is a form of electricity. Lightning can set fires, burn skin, electrocute things, cause explosions, and be generally destructive.

Lightning and thunder happen at the same time, but the speed of light (lightning) is so much faster than the speed of sound (thunder)—about a million times faster. That's why thunder always follows lightning. You see the flash of lightning instantly, and then, depending on how far away it is, you hear the thunder, which takes about five seconds to travel a mile.

Benjamin Franklin discovered Lightning a form of electricity

A Man struck (electrocuted) by Lightning

Thunder tries to catch up but is always behind. Lightning is the big boss. So, shouldn't such marvelous events of nature be called Lightning Storms instead of Thunderstorms?

At any rate, nah! Nope! Wouldn't wanna be a transformer pole like Rodney. I just wanna be me: a neighborhood streetlight.

"Don't worry, Junior. You're a natural for the job, but you're no ordinary streetlight. You're much more! You'll see. Just as long as you stay safe and healthy, you're gonna work far longer than I did. You don't need any pointers. It's an important and good job, and you'll get the hang of it in no time."

Thunder always following behind

Lightning the big boss

R.J.'s Day Begins

Pops was right! Working the job was natural for me. Once I adjusted to the hours and everything else, the job was easy as pie. Speaking of hours, it'll be dawn soon. The sun will rise, bringing bright sunlight. It will be daylight and time for me to get some shut-eye and rest.

Oh! Did you get that, huh? That I'm nocturnal, like the owl. I sleep and rest during daylight hours, from dawn to dusk, and do most of my activities and work during the dark hours of night, from dusk to dawn. Well, that's usually the case—except for a few times. Someone crossed my wires or accidentally flicked my switch on, and I ended up working in broad daylight, all day and all night long. Mind you, that's happened only a few times. Still, it's really annoying and such a waste of energy. But don't worry, I'm strong and able. It was a breeze. I handled the extra duty like a champ. Oh! But right now, here comes dawn and the sunlight.

At first, the glare of the sunlight used to really bother me. The brightness kept me from resting comfortably. Unlike the owl, I wasn't able to fly off to a dark hole in a tree, the darkness of a secluded belfry, or any shaded haven to escape the glare of daylight. But I was able to adjust. Soon, I got used to the brightness. I would turn my dome light off and just chill, and I was able to rest easy. Then I discovered that the glare of the sunlight would be the least of the things to interrupt my sleep.

The bright glare of sunlight

Two Early Intrusions
(Percy Pigeon and Tail-less Tobie)

Plick, plick! Plick, plick! Ya hear that? That's Percy Pigeon and his team of birds. I don't know why they have to roost on my dome. I don't know whether they do it just to mess with me or if they use my dome as a rest stop between flights. But that's not the worst of it.

It's bad when I hear, "Splat, splat!" That's the sound of bird poop dropping on my dome. Sometimes it splashes down the sides of my pole. That's so disgusting! It makes me want to puke.

Oh no! Here comes another disturbance.

Percy Pigeon with his kitte of Pigeons

Here comes Tobie Tail-less. We call him that 'cause there's just a two-inch stub where his tail should be. I don't know whether he bit it off himself, lost it in a dog fight, or if the wheel of a car rolled over his tail and snipped it off.

Gross! He's raising that leg and peeing on me.

"Tobie! Stop! I'm not a fire plug! I don't need irrigation. Go find some grass or a tree to irrigate."

But then I wonder: does pee—I mean urine—do the same thing as water? Does it irrigate for growth, or does it irritate growth? I don't know, and I don't really care. Just go find somewhere else to pee. Anyplace except on me. Scram! Get away!

Tobie Tail-less urinates on R.J.

Gooey Sticky Tape on R. J.

Whew! It's been quiet the last few hours, but now I hear old man Thomas coming down the street. I hear his cane tapping on the sidewalk.

What's that in his hand? Not another one! A flyer! I hate when people post signs on my pole advertising lawn and garage sales, upcoming events, lost pets—whatever. They never come back to take them down, even when others deface them or rip them to pieces. They just leave the signs there until they're weather-worn enough to disintegrate. But that usually leaves my pole feeling sticky and gooey from the glue on the tape.

Let's see. What does Mr. Thomas' flyer say?

"Missing: Spike, a White Spotted Brown Miniature Scotch Terrier; $100 Reward for Return."

Mr. Thomas' flyer taped to R.J.

Wow! Spike has been missing for more than two months. Mr. Thomas hasn't given up looking for him. Spike is long gone—either taken or hit by a car. In fact, my buddy a few blocks east of here says he thinks it was Spike he saw hit by a Range Rover. Spike didn't have a name tag, but a dog pound truck picked him up and took him away. I don't think Mr. Thomas will ever see Spike again.

Except for his white pelage (fur), Spike looks like a miniature version of Tobie. Maybe it would be nice if Mr. Thomas adopted Tobie. Tobie needs a good home. They would be a good combination—good for each other. It's just a thought.

MR. THOMAS + TOBIE → GOOD COMBINATION
GOOD FOR EACH OTHER

Bobby and the Crew Antics

And now, here comes that spirited little gamer Bobby Crawford and his hangout crew. Those guys can never pass by me without at least one of them swinging around on me. Usually, if one swings, they all swing. They swing around and kick my base, sometimes leaving scuff marks on me. Just four of them today; that's a relief.

Hey! One of those little bean-heads snatched down Mr. Thomas' flyer. He ripped it to pieces, mushed the pieces into a ball, and then threw it on the ground. Little bean-head, that's not a nice thing to do.

Oh, look! One of them is trying to climb my pole. I always get a kick and a laugh out of this.

Bobby Crawford and crew always swing around on R.J.

Bobby always challenges a new guy in the crew to climb my pole and touch the top of my light dome. None of his guys have ever done it—not in a million tries! It's a real struggle trying to climb my pole. It's exhausting! Ya see, I'm a little too slick for them. Once they scoot up my pole so far, their strength and energy give out. Their hands and feet slip, they lose their grip, and down they come, sliding back to the ground.

Watch out! Here comes the New Guy already. Slip! Zip! BAM! Ha, ha! Ha, ha! Oops! He landed on his "gluteus maximus." That's his butt. The other two crew guys cracked up. They pointed at the New Guy sitting on the ground and just laughed and laughed and laughed.

I'm a little too slick for you!

The Crew's Good Deeds

At least Bobby checked to see if the New Guy was okay and made sure he wasn't seriously hurt. Bobby is a cool guy like that. Most of the time, Bobby is a real sweetheart. That means Bobby is usually a kind and helpful person, like the time he organized his crew and all the fourth-grade boys to help with the book, flower, and plant fair. It was a school fundraiser project. They all volunteered.

Bobby set up and operated a wagon tow service. The boys would escort customers around the fair so customers could place purchased items in their wagons. When finished, they would transport the goods to the customers' cars. The fair and the wagon tow service were a big success! And thanks to tips from generous customers, it ended up being a little profitable for the boys.

Bobby and his crew do another really good thing. As much as they can, they try to make sure there's no bullying on the school playground or in their school. That's really terrific!

BOOK AND FLOWER FAIR
Tips for the help!

Who Can Hit R. J.'s Dome?

Still, at other times, they can be real knuckleheads—like now. Duck! Oh, I forgot. I can't duck. Those little gremlins are chucking rocks, trying to see who can hit my dome. I realize they're just little kids, but don't they know how dangerous it is to throw rocks—at anything, anybody, and especially me?

They throw the rocks up. The rocks could drop back down and hit them on the head or in the face. Little rock fragments could fall into their eyes. They could even break my light, and then glass splinters could fall into their eyes. It's good that, for the most part, they aren't strong enough to throw a rock high enough to reach my dome.

Imagine—they could put my light out. My light is the most important part of my job. But ya know, one time, even though my light wasn't broken, it was out for about three long months.

They are throwing rocks at R.J.'s light dome

R J.'s Three Month Outage
(The Home Invasion)

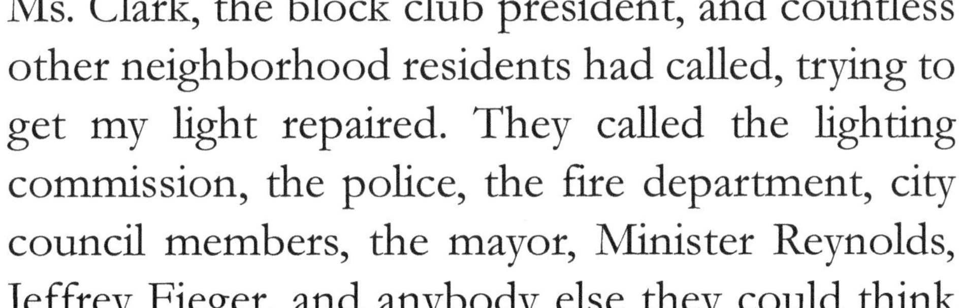

Ms. Clark, the block club president, and countless other neighborhood residents had called, trying to get my light repaired. They called the lighting commission, the police, the fire department, city council members, the mayor, Minister Reynolds, Jeffrey Fieger, and anybody else they could think of to help get my light back on. They even thought about calling the governor. Nothing worked.

So, for three long months, in the dark night hours from dusk to dawn, there I stood—helpless and fearful, unable to do my job. I felt sick. Then it happened during this time on a really dark night. Yep! You guessed it. The worst thing ever happened.

It was a really dark night because thick storm clouds blotted out any light from the moon and stars. It was pitch black, even though it was only 8:30 p.m. Mrs. Murray and her granddaughter Kayla were returning home from the church bazaar, bags of prizes and goodies on each arm.

It was so dark that they couldn't see those two really bad perps hiding behind the bushes at the side of the house. As Mrs. Murray unlocked her door, the perps jumped onto the porch, pounced on the two females, and forced them into the house, closing the door behind them.

The Robbers hid behind the bushes

Once inside the house, the perps gagged and bound Mrs. Murray and her granddaughter, then commenced to rob them. They stole TVs, computers, other electronic devices, jewelry, and money. They loaded their loot into a black van. I stood by helpless, feeling responsible as they cleaned Mrs. Murray out.

When they returned to collect the last of their haul, the two thugs paused and stared at Mrs. Murray and her granddaughter. I don't know if they were trying to intimidate the two females or what was on their minds. I couldn't take it anymore. I felt totally responsible for what was happening. I just couldn't stand by, watching and doing nothing. I had to do something to help Mrs. Murray.

With all my might and energy, I mustered up enough power to make my light blink. Blink! Blink! Blink! Blink! On! Off! On! Off! I blinked my light so hard that sparks flew everywhere from my dome. The wires leading to my dome crackled and sizzled like they were about to catch fire and explode.

The blinking lights and the popping and cracking sounds made by the wires must have frightened the robbers. They bolted out of Mrs. Murray's house, jumped into the black van, and took off like a bat out of H***. Well, you know where. Anyway, they sped off, leaving the door wide open.

Kayla and Grandmother Murray bound and tied up

It wasn't much, and perhaps it was a little late, but I think what I did may have saved Mrs. Murray and her granddaughter from a far worse fate. Those miserable creeps were caught a few weeks after robbing Mrs. Murray. It was discovered that they had committed several home invasions and break-ins. In three instances, other female victims had been raped as well as robbed. At least I was able to spare Mrs. Murray and Kayla from that ordeal.

One good thing did come from their frightful incident. The very next day, the lighting company came out—without even one call. They put in a new light, brand-new wires, and cleaned off my dome and pole. I looked and felt spanking brand new. I was healthy again and ready to work. I was so happy! I hope nothing like this ever happens to me again.

So all I'm sayin' is... "Help! Help!" Would somebody please stop these knuckle-headed kids from throwing rocks at my dome? One of them might get lucky and put my light out again, and we can't have that. It's just not safe!

Wishing I Was a Track Star

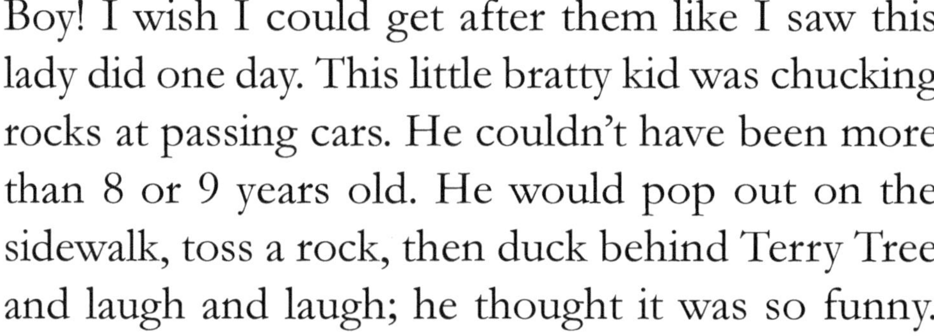

Boy! I wish I could get after them like I saw this lady did one day. This little bratty kid was chucking rocks at passing cars. He couldn't have been more than 8 or 9 years old. He would pop out on the sidewalk, toss a rock, then duck behind Terry Tree and laugh and laugh; he thought it was so funny. Most drivers would yell out a few obscenities, but they would keep on driving. Not this one lady!

Tossed a rock through an open car window

That little bugger threw a rock, and it went through an open car window. It almost hit the lady in the face. She slammed on the brakes and shifted gears to park. Leaving the door wide open, she dashed out of the car and took off after that menacing kid. The little boy was so startled that he stood there frozen for a second or two, but then he took off running.

That lady was like a track star! She ran him down and caught him. She took a lanyard, which held some keys and a whistle, from around her neck and whipped his butt and legs. She wore that little fanny out! When she finally cut him loose, he took off crying and running. She yelled after him, "Yeah! You better run home. Uh-huh! Tell ya mama! If she wants to talk to me, tell her I'll be at the Rec Center. I'd really like to talk to her!"

Like a track star, the lady ran him down

Turns out, the lady was the Playleader at the Rec Center a couple of blocks away. She probably scared the bejesus out of that little kid! Don't know whether he ever threw rocks at cars again. If he did, it wasn't around here.

If only I could be like that lady and get after those little rogues chunking rocks at my dome.

Help, somebody! They're still at it!

Reynolds and Lewis on the Scene

If only I could be like that lady and get after those little munchkins, 'cause they're still throwing rocks at me. Help! Somebody, anybody, please… Oh! They're running away, scattering in different directions. No wonder! I see Reverend Reynolds and Officer Lewis coming up the street, headed this way. Bobby and his boys know they shouldn't be throwing rocks, so they scurried off like jackrabbits.

Litter bug! Litter bug! Litter bug! Litter bug! You know what a litter bug is? A litter bug is a person who carelessly drops litter in a public area. Litter is trash—any kind of waste. Well, Bobby and his boys just took off and left soda and juice bottles, a soda pop can, and other waste on the sidewalk and in the street. Those guys are a bunch of rock-throwing litter bugs.

They scattered ran off in different directions

Wait a minute! Wait a minute! Officer Lewis and Reverend Reynolds have passed by, and here comes Bobby Crawford with a plastic garbage bag in hand. Surprise! Surprise! Bobby is cleaning up the scene.

I take it all back. I guess Bobby Crawford and company are not a bunch of litter bugs. But that rock-throwing matter still needs to be addressed. At least they didn't cause any damage or harm this time, but they need to learn and understand that it's unsafe to throw rocks at windows, cars, me, or anything. Should they continue this errant behavior of throwing rocks and cause any damage or harm, then they should expect "just deserts" for their wayward actions.

Stuck to a Lamp Post
(How'd It Taste)

Speaking of just deserts, one of those little bean heads received just deserts for doing something he shouldn't have done. It wasn't Bobby, but one of his boys—Monte. It was just last winter. My friend Jason, the lamp post down the way at the school bus stop, told me about what happened.

It was a very, very cold day with subzero temperatures. Brrr! Everything was frosted and coated with ice—including Jason. Monte decided to lick the lamp post. Don't know why! Don't know whether he was just curious and wanted to taste the ice on Jason or whether one of the kids dared him to do it. Monte knew it was something he shouldn't have done—licking a pole, icy or not—but he did it anyway.

That kid's tongue got stuck to the lamp post. Like a stamp on a letter, he couldn't pull it loose. He was moaning and groaning: "Agh, agh, agh, agh!" Trying to say something, but nobody could understand what he was trying to say.

The other kids waiting at the bus stop just laughed and laughed and laughed. None of them even tried to help him. They didn't know what to do anyway.

Licking that frozen pole was like licking a piece of hot ice. It's called hot ice for a reason. It's icy to keep things cold and frozen, but if it stays in contact with the skin, it will cause frostbite, which feels like a hot burning sensation. The skin will blister and swell as if it has been burned by something hot.

One of the kids went to tell Ms. Clark, who lives near the bus stop, what was going on. Ms. Clark brought out a pitcher of cool water and poured it on the pole where Monte's tongue was stuck. Jason released his tongue.

His tongue stuck to the frozen lamp post

Monte's "just deserts" for licking that frozen pole was having a blistered and swollen tongue for a couple of days. Pretty sure he won't do that again. He learned a lesson about licking a frozen pole, but he has lessons yet to learn. Monte is the one who snatched down Mr. Thomas' flyer and was one of the knuckleheads chunking rocks at my dome. He's just a little kid, but I'm sure he'll learn not to do unkind and unsafe acts without facing some real hard knocks.

At least when those little bean heads saw Reverend Reynolds and Officer Lewis coming up the street, they stopped throwing rocks at me and ran off. The fact that they ran away shows that they know throwing rocks is wrong. They're gone now, so I won't worry about that anymore. I just need to get a few winks before it's time for work.

Startled Awake!
(A Bike Collision)

ZZZZZZZ!

I was resting easy, until I heard someone shout,
"Watch out!"

Startled awake, I opened my eyes just in time to see Nikki swerve hard to the left to keep from running over Baby J. Having heard the ice cream truck's jingle, Baby J had pulled away from his mother's grasp and run straight toward the sound. He darted right in front of Nikki, who is just learning to ride a two-wheeler. She did everything she could to avoid hitting and running over Baby J.

Baby J runs toward sound of ice cream truck jingle

Wham! Nikki runs full speed into me. There was a loud clanging sound as the handlebars of her bike crashed into my pole. The sudden stop and impact threw Nikki up and almost flipped her forward over the handlebars. She came slamming down onto the handlebars, and she and the bike crashed to the ground. It's a good thing she's wearing all that protective gear—helmet, elbow pads, knee pads—otherwise, she might have been seriously injured.

Me? Oh, I'm all right! Not a scratch or a dent. Just a little blemish where the handlebars rubbed against my pole. But I did feel a slight vibration and heard a banging sound all the way up to my dome when we collided. Other than that, I'm just fine. Ya know, I was made to withstand high impact, even though that wasn't much of an impact. Still, I consider myself pretty lucky when I think about the impact my pals Jerry and Deante had experienced.

Nikki crashes into R.J.

High Impact for Jerry and Deante
(Crunch and Boom)

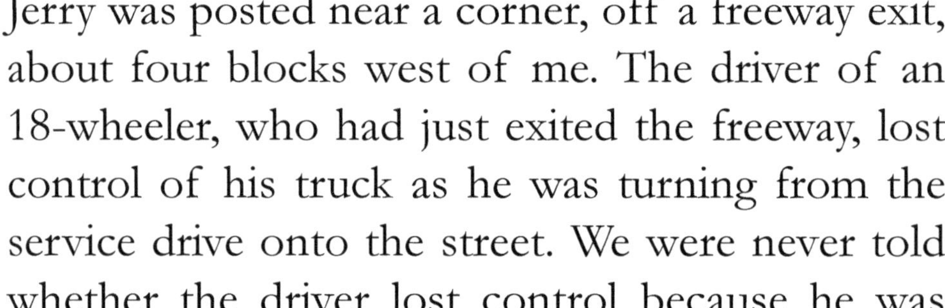

Jerry was posted near a corner, off a freeway exit, about four blocks west of me. The driver of an 18-wheeler, who had just exited the freeway, lost control of his truck as he was turning from the service drive onto the street. We were never told whether the driver lost control because he was drunk, speeding to catch the traffic light, fell asleep while driving, or had a medical emergency.

Anyway, that truck plowed into Jerry, jackknifed, and plowed into him again. Crunch! Now that was a high impact!

The truck driver was lucky; he survived with just a few scratches and bruises. But not Jerry! Jerry was bent. I mean really bent. He was so bent that people could swing on his pole near his dome just by jumping a few inches off the ground.

And that's exactly what they did—swing on his pole, especially the kids. That was a dangerous situation, so within the next couple of days, they took Jerry away, and I haven't seen him since.

Swinging on Jerry's bent pole

Of course, my friend Deante suffered another kind of high impact. He's one of those lamp posts that house a control unit at the base. One day, somebody removed his panel and set off an explosive device inside the cavity of his base.

BOOM!

The fire-resistant wires only burned partially, so they pulled his wires out and cut them into pieces. Somebody caused a blackout. But Deante withstood the impact of the blast.

He survived the impact. You could see the scars and scorch marks on his pole and control unit. He wasn't working, but he was still standing. He was out of commission for a while, but they must have rewired him. He looks a little battle-worn, but his dome light is working just fine.

What happened to Deante, Jerry, and the robbery at Mrs. Murray's house makes it perfectly clear what my dad meant when he said, "As long as you stay safe and healthy…"

Scorch marks left after bomb exploded

A Freeway Lamp Post: To Be or Not to Be

That's why I sometimes wish I was a freeway lamp post. Freeway lamp posts have it "made in the shade." That's just an expression, of course, because they're hardly ever in the shade. But they do have it pretty easy.

A freeway lamp post is way up high. Its base rests on a concrete wall at least 3 to 4 feet high; so there's little chance that anything would crash into it. No doubt it's safer and probably healthier too, but then the life of a freeway lamp post is far less interesting and eventful.

Traffic just zips by. Every once in a while, a really cool motorcycle might flash by. But then, it's just a fleeting glance. Things do slow down when there's an accident, a multi-car pileup, traffic jams, or backups. Sure, that might be interesting, but who wants to deal with a bunch of frustrated, aggravated, grumpy, unfriendly types? Freeway lamp posts also oversee the service drive, but there's even less activity there.

Being a freeway lamp post can be pretty boring. That's not for me.

I'm glad to be where I am and do what I do. Like my father said, it's an important and good job, and I do it well!

It's about two and a half hours to dusk. I'm not going to be able to do anything if I don't get a little more rest. That'll do me right! I'll take a little snooze before the big show. When my light flicks on, I'll be ready and raring to go.

Taffic back-up on freeway

The Hours from Dusk to Dawn Begin

Flick! My light is on, and I'm ready to go.

The first hour or two is kinda slow and calm. Folks are finishing dinner and just chillin'. Things will be happening soon. In fact, here comes the gambling crew now. I wasn't expecting them tonight. They use my light to get their game on. They bring a flat board, like an upside-down tabletop, and they play craps on it.

Craps is a dice game. You bet money. You win, or you lose. Craps has its own language, like boxcars, snake eyes, and seven the hard way. It's exciting to watch them play, but I don't think they should be playing craps because there are always too many arguments and sometimes fights. It seems everybody wants to play and gamble, but nobody wants to lose their money. That doesn't seem to be Keith's problem tonight—losing, that is.

Keith has been really lucky tonight, and he just had a run of seven straight passes. I think that means he threw a seven or eleven on his first throw of the dice. His fists and pockets are bulging with dollars. He's the big winner tonight, and he's ready to split.

Keith passes the dice to another player and stands up.

"Hey, man!" one of the guys yells. "I know you ain't 'bout to leave without givin' us a chance to win back some of our money."

Keith froze in his tracks.

Jo-Jo comes running up, panting and out of breath. "The cops are coming! The cops are coming!"

They use R.J.'s light to get their game on

Big Tony snatches up the craps board, points a finger at Keith, and disappears into the dark of night with the rest of the crew. Keith stays for an extra moment, folds the bills in his hand, and puts them in his pocket.

As the police car rolls up, the cop says, "Hey, Keith! It's a little late, man. You need to get on home now."

"I'm headed that way now!" Keith answers as he heads off home in the opposite direction from the crew.

Ever since those crooks robbed Mrs. Murray, the cops have been randomly patrolling the neighborhood. Lucky for Keith, the police showed up when they did. He was able to escape with his big winnings.

Policeman says, "It's past curfew"
POLICE
"I'm headed home now, Sir." says Keith

A Clandestine Meeting Point

I know it's nearly midnight because Marcus is leaning on my pole. Marcus is waiting for Mia. Mia can see Marcus from her upstairs bedroom window. Two or three nights a week, after everyone in her house is asleep, Mia sneaks out to meet Marcus at my pole—usually a little after midnight.

I don't think it's right. Marcus is 20, and Mia is only 16. If only her parents knew why Mia seemed so tired some mornings. Marcus and Mia hang out for a couple of hours, but they don't stay at my pole for long. It's too bright. They go down the block to Terry Tree, whose wide bark, branches, and leaves shield them from the light. There, they can smooch in private. But I am so relieved when Mia is back home.

Mia and Marcus hanging out at Terry tree

Uh! Oh!

The wise old owl has been watching the whole time. He knows that Marcus should not be meeting with Mia this late. Marcus wants to keep it a secret. It's not a good idea, and it is not safe for Mia. Mia's parents surely would not approve.

Oh! Oh! I can see it from here.

As Mia is climbing back through her window, her bedroom light flicks on. Mia is caught! Her mom was waiting in the dark for her to return. Wildly shaking and pointing her finger at Mia, her mom is reading her the riot act. I can hear all that fussing and commotion all the way down here. I hope her mom doesn't wake the neighborhood.

But you know, maybe it's good that Mia got caught before she got herself into real trouble. She's only 16! Hurray! These late night meetings should end. Mia will be safer.

Mia is caught climbing back through bedroom window

Hopeful for Parker

It has been pretty quiet the past two hours, but here comes Parker, the neighborhood drunk, staggering and stumbling down the street. He can barely walk.

Watch out for that raised slab of concrete in the sidewalk.

Oops! He tripped. He's going to fall on his face. Whew! That was close. He catches himself on my pole before he smashes his face on the ground. I'll hold him up for fifteen or twenty minutes or so until he can get himself together and move on. But you know, the same thing happened three weeks ago—only worse.

It was a Saturday night. Parker stumbled and fell into me. I held him up for almost half an hour before he was able to move on. But then something happened to him. He was held up for real. I mean robbed.

A couple of blocks after he left me, two thugs jumped him, beat him down, and took what little money he had. He was in the hospital for two weeks.

And here he is, back at it again. Parker is a sitting duck—an easy target for muggers and thieves. I guess that's the chance you take when you get so drunk that you can hardly walk.

I hope he makes it home safe and sound.

R.J. trying to hold up Parker

The Dawning of Happy Day

Uh-huh! Like clockwork, there is Mr. Davis pulling into his driveway. Mr. Davis is the late-night supervisor at Walmart. His shift ends at 5:00 a.m., and every morning after work, he arrives home at exactly 6:00 a.m. It's a sure sign that dawn isn't far off.

To the east, I can see a faint light in the sky.

Hooray! The sun is rising. Dawn is here! And guess what? Today is Sunday! I can turn off my light and get a few winks before the church bells ring.

I don't mind church bells ringing. In fact, I love it when church bells ring.

The sun is rising in the east

People come to church and sing. Preachers preach. Everything is so uplifting and inspiring. I really enjoy listening to the good-spirited, happy music and a good sermon or two. I get a chance to be thankful for my safety and good health. I also get the chance to pray for the safety and health of all those in my domain, especially Tobie, Deante, Mia, and Parker.

Everything is usually calmer on Sundays, so there is time for me to get plenty of rest, even with church and all: ringing bells, tambourines, pianos, organs, drums banging; choirs singing, raising their voices in praise.

Sundays are great. Sunday is a happy day.

Choirs sing good-spirited, uplifting songs

I have to get ready for happy day. It's been great talking to you, but I have to go now. Perhaps you can come back again some other time. I'll be able to tell you more about what happens in my life. You can always find me, 'cause right here is where I'll always be. See ya then. Later!